What's It Like Out?

Hurricane!

Kris Hirschmann

ABDO
Publishing Company

551.552
Hirschmann

visit us at
www.abdopublishing.com

Published by ABDO Publishing Company, 8000 West 78th Street, Edina, Minnesota 55439.
Copyright © 2008 by Abdo Consulting Group, Inc. International copyrights reserved in all
countries. No part of this book may be reproduced in any form without written permission from the
publisher. The Checkerboard Library™ is a trademark and logo of ABDO Publishing Company.

Printed in the United States.

Cover Photo: iStockphoto
Interior Photos: AP Images pp. 19, 20, 27; Comstock p. 4; FEMA News Photo p. 24; iStockphoto
    pp. 1, 13, 28, 29; NASA/NOAA p. 14; National Oceanic and Atmospheric
    Administration/Department of Commerce pp. 11, 21; Peter Arnold p. 10; Photo Researchers,
    Inc. pp. 7, 22; Robert Simmon/NASA GSFC p. 9; U.S. Navy pp. 23, 25; UW-CIMSS/SSEC
    p. 27; Visible Earth/NASA pp. 5, 6, 13

Image on page 17 reprinted with permission from *Encyclopædia Britannica*, © 2005 by
    Encyclopædia Britannica, Inc.

Series Coordinator: Megan M. Gunderson
Editors: Megan M. Gunderson, BreAnn Rumsch
Art Direction & Cover Design: Neil Klinepier

Library of Congress Cataloging-in-Publication Data

Hirschmann, Kris, 1967-
  Hurricane! / Kris Hirschmann.
       p. cm. -- (What's it like out?)
  Includes bibliographical references and index.
  ISBN 978-1-59928-942-7
  1. Hurricanes--Juvenile literature. I. Title.

  QC944.2.H569 2008
  551.55'2--dc22
                                2007029154

Contents

Hurricane!

How much do you know about these powerful storms?

One summer morning, you wake up to find rain pelting your window. The skies are cloudy and dark. Trees whip back and forth in the wind. "I won't be playing outside today," you think.

But five minutes later, the wind has died down and the rain is gone. "Hooray!" you say. You jump out of bed and start to get dressed. Surprise! The rain and the wind soon return. What is happening outside?

Just then you hear a weather report on your radio. "Get ready for the big one, folks," says the forecaster. "We'll see some strange weather today as the storm rolls in." Aha! How could you forget? A hurricane is on its way!

Hurricanes, or tropical cyclones, are huge, spinning weather systems. They are the most powerful storms on Earth. The biggest hurricanes can knock down homes, flood cities, and harm thousands of people. Safety is key when these monster storms approach.

Hurricane Ophelia approaching the U.S. East Coast in 2005

Where Tropical Cyclones Occur

Tropical cyclones are known by different names depending on where they occur. Storms in the North Atlantic and eastern North Pacific oceans are called hurricanes. Storms occurring in the western North Pacific are called typhoons. In the Indian Ocean and the western South Pacific, these storms are called severe tropical cyclones, tropical cyclones, or just cyclones.

Tropical cyclones always get started near the equator. Why?

Orange indicates that the sea surface temperature is at or above 82 degrees Fahrenheit (28°C). There, the seas are warm enough to fuel a hurricane.

These storms run partly on heat, just as a car runs on gasoline. The sun's rays hit the **tropics** very directly. In the northern **hemisphere**, the year's maximum **solar radiation** has been received by June 22. Tropical seas get warmer and warmer, reaching their peak a few weeks later.

Finally, the water reaches 80 degrees Fahrenheit (26.5°C) to a depth of at least 150 feet (50 m). It is then warm enough to power a hurricane.

Some seas are cold all year long. For example, the Southern and Arctic oceans never reach hurricane temperatures. So, tropical cyclones do not occur in these regions.

Hurricane Frequency

The Pacific Ocean sees the largest number of tropical cyclones. The Indian Ocean ranks second in number of tropical cyclones, followed by the Atlantic Ocean.

In the United States, hurricanes are more likely to hit Florida than any other state. Texas sees the second-largest number of hits, followed by Louisiana and North Carolina.

Hurricane Season

Tropical cyclones are most common after an ocean reaches its peak temperature. The warm stretch when most hurricanes form is called hurricane season.

Water temperatures peak at different times around the world. So, hurricane season changes from place to place. For example, the Atlantic hurricane season officially lasts from June 1 to November 30. August, September, and October are the season's most active months.

On average, 11 tropical storms form each year over the Atlantic Ocean, the Caribbean Sea, and the Gulf of Mexico. Typically, six of them become hurricanes. An average of five hurricanes make **landfall** in the United States every three years.

The Northwest Pacific **basin** storm season is longer than the Atlantic season. There, typhoons can occur at any time of the year. The main season lasts from July to November. It peaks in late August or early September. The Northeast Pacific basin sees hurricanes from May to November.

In the Southwest Indian **basin**, tropical cyclones are common from October through May. The Southeast Indian/Australian basin and the Australian/Southwest Pacific basin also see tropical cyclones from October to May. The North Indian basin has two tropical cyclone season peaks. There, tropical cyclones occur from April to December, with peaks in May and November.

Hurricane Seasons

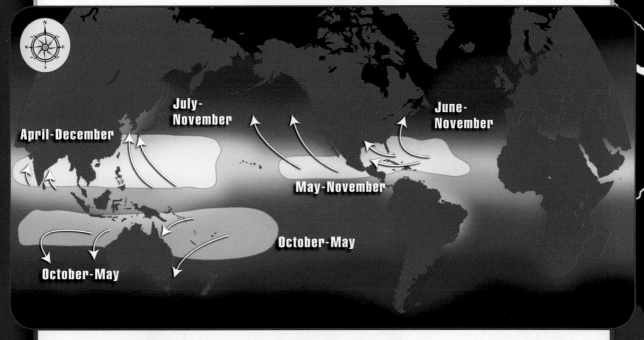

The Wind Picks Up

Ocean water is not the only thing that warms up during the summer months. The air heats up, too. This happens because of **evaporation**. As the water warms up, tiny

particles called molecules gain energy. They bounce around quickly and break free of the water's surface.

The moisture, or water vapor, in the air rises and cools. When it cools, it **condenses** to form clouds and releases heat to warm the atmosphere. Warm air exerts less pressure than cold air, which is **dense** and heavy. Pressure differences try to even themselves out. So, air from high-pressure areas rushes toward low-pressure areas. We feel this movement as wind.

For a hurricane to form, high-pressure areas must surround a low-pressure core. In these places, air near ground level rushes inward from all directions. The winds head toward a central point. There, they begin the warming process and start to rise, too. The air blasts upward, carrying more ocean moisture with it. As the rising moisture cools and forms clouds, the sky darkens.

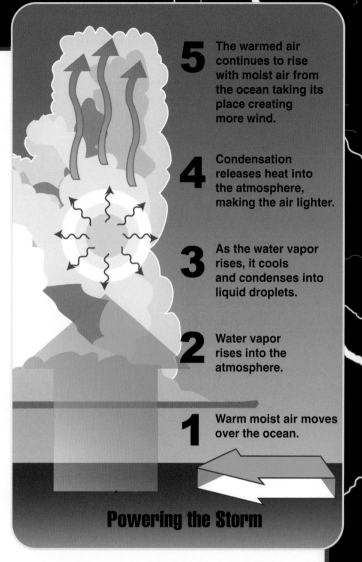

5 The warmed air continues to rise with moist air from the ocean taking its place creating more wind.

4 Condensation releases heat into the atmosphere, making the air lighter.

3 As the water vapor rises, it cools and condenses into liquid droplets.

2 Water vapor rises into the atmosphere.

1 Warm moist air moves over the ocean.

Powering the Storm

An area where rain clouds are forming at sea is called a tropical disturbance. If there is enough rising heat and moisture, conditions may be right for hurricane formation.

A Storm Takes Shape

What happens next depends on the weather conditions. Strong wind shear, or change in wind speed with altitude, may rip apart the rising air column. But if the wind speed does not change much with altitude, the air keeps rising straight up. This helps keep the cycle going.

Upper-level winds now enter the picture. If these winds are strong, they act like a lid on the column of air. Without anywhere to go, the system of rising air is **disrupted**. But if the winds are light, the rising air is fanned outward in all directions. This allows more rising air to take its place. These conditions help fuel the cycle.

As more air rises, the pressure continues lowering. The more the pressure lowers, the faster the air rushes in toward the system's center. Low-level winds pick up as more air flows toward the storm's core.

Around this time, the entire storm system may start to spin. The Coriolis effect **deflects** the winds as they travel inward toward the low-pressure core. As wind speed picks up, the storm system rotates faster and faster.

The Coriolis effect describes how Earth's rotation affects the way things travel across the planet. Because of the Coriolis effect, tropical cyclones that form north of the equator spin counterclockwise. Those that form south of the equator spin clockwise.

Like an ice-skater pulling in her arms, the winds become faster the closer they get to the center.

A Hurricane Is Born

A rotating tropical disturbance gets a new name when its wind speed measures 23 miles per hour (36 km/h). The storm is now called a tropical depression. The depression is cloudy and stormy. Its winds blow at speeds of up to 39 miles per hour (63 km/h).

If conditions are good for hurricane formation, the winds in the depression pick up. When wind speeds reach more

In 2005, Tropical Storm Alpha followed Hurricane Wilma.

Naming the Storm

Storms that reach tropical storm strength are given names. In the United States, there are six lists of names for Atlantic storms and six for Pacific storms. These are rotated, so every six years the same list is used again.

The names alternate alphabetically between male and female. If a year's names are all used, the following storms are named according to the Greek alphabet, which starts with alpha. The letters *q*, *u*, *x*, *y*, and *z* are not included because so few names begin with those letters. Other areas of the world use separate lists of names or numbers to label hurricanes in their region.

If a particularly destructive hurricane occurs, that name is generally taken off the list, or retired. A new name is then chosen to replace it in the rotation. For example, Katia replaced Katrina after the 2005 hurricane season. Retirement and replacement of names are decided at meetings of the World Meteorological Organization.

than 39 miles per hour (63 km/h), the system is **upgraded** again. Now, it is considered a tropical storm. The system forms a circular shape as winds blast inward at greater and greater speeds.

The growing storm sucks available heat and moisture from the sea. It becomes more powerful as it absorbs this fuel. Eventually, its wind speeds exceed 74 miles per hour (119 km/h). At this point, the system officially becomes a hurricane. The **trade winds** push the spinning monster storm westward across the sea.

Anatomy of a Hurricane

The newborn hurricane is like a huge, hungry vacuum. It sucks in heat and moisture from the sea. This material spirals in to the storm's center. As the storm strengthens, it organizes itself into paths called rainbands. Conditions are windy and stormy inside the bands, but calmer between them.

The rainbands are loose near a hurricane's edges. As these bands pass overhead, the weather changes from bad to good and back again. But, the bands squeeze together toward the middle of the storm. As a result, the calm patches get shorter. The periods of wind and rain **intensify** and last longer.

Finally the raging winds approach the hurricane's center. There, the strongest winds and rain are located in a roaring tube called the eyewall. The eyewall's weather is incredibly violent.

However, the area inside the tube is almost windless. This area is called the eye. It stretches all the way from the sea to the sky. From above, it looks like a round hole in a thick blanket of clouds.

On average, hurricanes are about 300 miles (500 km) wide. The eye is usually 10 to 40 miles (16 to 64 km) across.

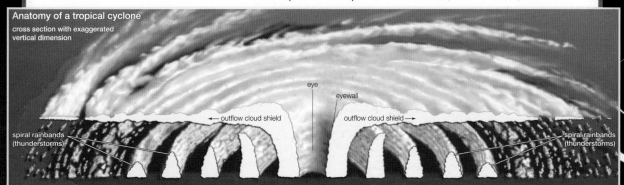

Anatomy of a tropical cyclone
cross section with exaggerated vertical dimension

eye
eyewall
← outflow cloud shield
outflow cloud shield →
spiral rainbands (thunderstorms)
spiral rainbands (thunderstorms)

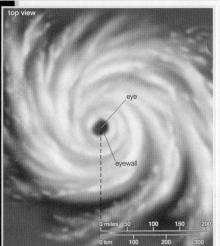

top view

eye
eyewall

0 miles 50 100 150 200
0 km 100 200 300

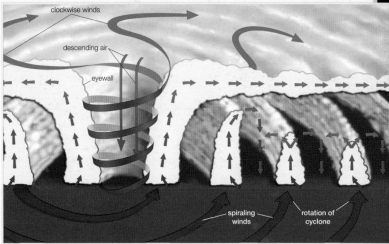

clockwise winds
descending air
eyewall
spiraling winds
rotation of cyclone

Measuring Hurricanes

Newly formed hurricanes are powerful storms. But, they may become even more powerful in certain conditions. Scientists use a tool called the Saffir-Simpson hurricane scale to describe a hurricane's **intensity**.

The Saffir-Simpson hurricane scale has five categories. Hurricanes with wind speeds of 74 to 95 miles per hour (119 to 153 km/h) fall into Category 1. Hurricanes with wind speeds above 155 miles per hour (249 km/h) fall into Category 5. Category 2, 3, and 4 storms fall between these extremes.

In addition to wind speed, the Saffir-Simpson hurricane scale includes storm surge information. All hurricanes push a bulge of seawater as they travel. This pileup of water is the storm surge. Storm surge height is linked to a hurricane's wind speeds.

The Saffir-Simpson Hurricane Scale

Category 1 (74-95 mph)
Damage primarily to trees and unanchored mobile homes; some coastal flooding

Category 2 (96-110 mph)
Some damage to roofs, doors, windows, trees and shrubbery; flooding damage to piers

Category 3 (111-130 mph)
Some structural damage; large trees blown down; flooding near shoreline and possibly inland; mobile homes destroyed

Category 4 (131-155 mph)
Extensive damage to doors and windows; major damage to lower floors near shore; terrain may be flooded well inland

Category 5 (more than 155 mph)
Complete roof failure and some building failures; massive evacuation; flooding causes major damage to lower floors of all shoreline buildings

Herbert Saffir and Dr. Bob Simpson developed the Saffir-Simpson hurricane scale in 1969. It is used to rank hurricanes in the eastern North Pacific Ocean, the North Atlantic Ocean, the Caribbean Sea, and the Gulf of Mexico.

CATEGORY	WIND SPEED	STORM SURGE
1	74–95 mph (119–153 km/h)	4–5 feet (1.2–1.5 m)
2	96–110 mph (154–177 km/h)	6–8 feet (1.8–2.4 m)
3	111–130 mph (178–209 km/h)	9–12 feet (2.7–3.7 m)
4	131–155 mph (210–249 km/h)	13–18 feet (3.9–5.5 m)
5	More than 155 mph (>249 km/h)	More than 18 feet (>5.5 m)

Tracking the Storm

Whatever their category, all hurricanes are dangerous. So, scientists watch these systems carefully by using **satellites**, airplanes, and other tools. Scientists keep track of a hurricane's wind speeds. And, they try to guess where a hurricane is headed. To calculate a storm's possible path, they enter weather data into special computer programs.

Some storm paths curve harmlessly out to sea. But others

Scientists track tropical storms, too. As with hurricanes, watches and warnings are issued when these storms approach.

appear to be heading for land. When this is the case, scientists issue hurricane watches or warnings. A hurricane watch means the approaching storm might strike a specific area within 36 hours. A hurricane warning means the storm is

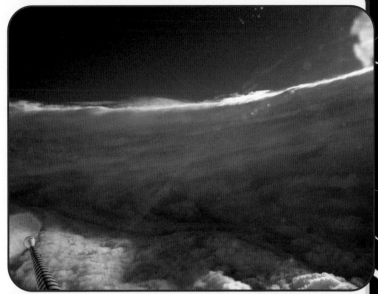

Hurricane hunters fly aircraft through hurricanes to gather information for scientists to study. In 2005, aircraft captured images of Hurricane Katrina's eyewall.

expected to strike an area within 24 hours.

Hurricane watches and warnings are very important. They give people time to prepare for the approaching storm. Some people do this by evacuating the area. Other people choose to stay and prepare to ride out the stormy weather. They board up their windows and buy flashlights, batteries, and groceries.

Making Landfall

The weather is usually calm 48 hours before a hurricane makes **landfall**. But about 24 hours before the storm hits, choppy whitecaps appear and grow on the seas. The surf gets rougher as the storm draws near.

Some scientists venture outdoors when a hurricane approaches. However, high winds and flying debris make it very dangerous to be outside during a hurricane.

Before long, the weather worsens to match the surf. The hurricane's outer rainbands appear. Winds pick up as the bands swirl overhead. The cloud cover thickens, and the skies darken. Lightning flashes, thunder crashes, and rain pours down.

Storm surge caused severe flooding during Hurricane Katrina in 2005.

Conditions become increasingly severe as the storm advances. The wind starts to shriek as its speed increases. Heavy rain floods the ground. At the same time, the storm surge arrives. Salty water gushes inland as the seas overflow.

The storm peaks as the eyewall reaches land. Winds may now be blasting at speeds of more than 150 miles per hour (240 km/h). But as the storm heads inland, these winds die off. Remember, a hurricane can't survive without fuel from the warm ocean waters. It soon falls apart, leaving a path of destruction in its wake.

Hurricane Damage

Hurricanes may weaken quickly over land. But, they do plenty of damage before they break up. Strong hurricanes can flatten buildings, cause dangerous flying debris, and blow down forests. They can destroy sheds, billboards, and anything else that gets in their way.

After a hurricane, there is often a lot of cleaning up to do. Everyone must watch for washed-out roads, check their homes for damage, and carefully remove debris.

Wind and waves can severely damage boats and even move them inland!

In coastal areas, a hurricane's storm surge can be even more deadly than its winds. The surge rolls in rapidly as the storm approaches. Wind-driven waves on top of the surge raise the water level even higher. Soon, the surge is deep enough to flow inland. It sweeps away homes, roads, and cars as it travels.

Flooding can also become a problem farther inland. A hurricane can dump huge amounts of rain onto the land. Rivers and storm drains overflow as the downpour continues. Sometimes, rainfall totals measure 20 to 40 inches (50 to 100 cm)!

The Big Ones

Several U.S. hurricanes have caused major floods. In 1928, an unnamed hurricane caused a lake surge in Florida's Lake Okeechobee. The lake's water level rose six to nine feet (2 to 3 m), causing severe flooding.

In 1935, the most **intense** hurricane to make **landfall** in the United States struck Florida. This Category 5 storm killed hundreds of **World War I veterans** working in the Florida Keys.

Hurricane Floyd's intense rainfall caused flooding from North Carolina to New York in 1999. Wilmington, North Carolina, received 19.06 inches (48.41 cm) of rain!

And in 2005, Hurricane Katrina damaged **levees** around New Orleans, Louisiana. Water poured over and through the levees, covering 80 percent of the city. Hundreds of residents died during this event.

In other storms, wind damage has caused memorable destruction. In 1989, Hurricane Hugo's winds blew through Charleston, South Carolina, at 100 miles per hour

Hurricane Katrina caused more than $75 billion in damage. It was the costliest storm in U.S. history.

(160 km/h). The storm uprooted trees and caused major damage in the city.

Hurricane Andrew tore into more than 100,000 south Florida buildings in August 1992. And a few weeks later, Hurricane Iniki swept across Kauai, Hawaii. The storm destroyed houses, tore down power and telephone lines, and left thousands of people homeless.

Be Prepared

Nothing can stop a hurricane's destruction. But, lives can be spared if people are ready for the storm. Experts recommend several simple steps to help families prepare for a hurricane.

Make sure your family's disaster supplies kit is ready. Your family car's gas tank should be full, in case you need to evacuate. And, make sure you have a place to meet if family members become separated.

Secure your home. Bring flower pots, wind chimes, and other small items indoors. Put boards over your windows to

Bottled water is a vital part of a disaster supplies kit. You should include one gallon (4 L) of water per person per day.

protect them from flying debris. If evacuating, an adult should turn off the water, electricity, and gas in your home.

Always listen to the radio or the television for weather updates and evacuation information. Evacuate immediately if you are told to do so.

If you do not need to evacuate, stay inside. Find a room with no windows. Stay there until you are sure the storm has passed. When the eye passes overhead, conditions briefly become calmer. So, make sure you stay inside until authorities have told you it is safe to leave.

Being prepared is the best way to protect yourself when a hurricane strikes. If a monster hurricane approaches, more people may be asked to evacuate. By going far away, they can protect themselves from nature's most powerful storms, hurricanes!

Adults should buy plywood ahead of time and cut each piece to fit your windows. That way, they will be able to easily install them if a storm heads your way!

Glossary

basin - a large area of the earth's surface covered by ocean.

condense - to change from a gas or a vapor into a liquid or a solid, usually caused by a decrease in temperature.

deflect - to turn something aside from a fixed or straight path.

dense - having a high mass per unit volume.

disrupt - to throw into disorder.

evaporation - changing from a liquid or a solid into a vapor.

hemisphere - one half of Earth.

intense - marked by great energy.

landfall - the approach to or the making of a landing.

levee - a ridge of earth built along a river to prevent flooding.

satellite - a manufactured object that orbits Earth. It relays weather and scientific information back to Earth.

solar radiation - energy given off by the sun.

trade winds - winds blowing toward the equator from 30 degrees north or south latitude. North of the equator, the winds blow from the northeast. South of the equator, they blow from the southeast.

tropics - an area extending 23.5 degrees north or south of Earth's equator.

upgrade - to increase or improve.

veteran - a person who has served in the armed forces.

World War I - from 1914 to 1918, fought in Europe. Great Britain, France, Russia, the United States, and their allies were on one side. Germany, Austria-Hungary, and their allies were on the other side.

Web Sites

To learn more about weather, visit ABDO Publishing Company on the World Wide Web at **www.abdopublishing.com**. Web sites about weather are featured on our Book Links page. These links are routinely monitored and updated to provide the most current information available.

Index